For Logan and Jake
—K. F.

For Maddy
—J. F.

SIMON & SCHUSTER BOOKS FOR YOUNG READERS • An imprint of Simon & Schuster Children's
Publishing Division • 1230 Avenue of the Americas, New York, New York 10020 • Text copyright © 2012 by Kate
Feiffer • Illustrations copyright © 2012 by Jules Feiffer • All rights reserved, including the right of reproduction in
whole or in part in any form. • SIMON & SCHUSTER BOOKS FOR YOUNG READERS is a trademark of Simon & Schuster, Inc. •
For information about special discounts for bulk purchases, please contact Simon & Schuster Special Sales at 1-866-506-1949
or business@simonandschuster.com. • The Simon & Schuster Speakers Bureau can bring authors to your live event. For more
information or to book an event, contact the Simon & Schuster Speakers Bureau at 1-866-248-3049 or visit our website at
www.simonspeakers.com. • Book design by Chloë Foglia • The text for this book is set in Garamond. • The illustrations for
this book are rendered in brush, ink, and watercolor markers. • Manufactured in China • 0312 SCP
10 9 8 7 6 5 4 3 2
Library of Congress Cataloging-in-Publication Data • Feiffer, Kate. • No go sleep! / Kate Feiffer ; illustrated by Jules
Feiffer. — 1st ed. • p. cm. • "A Paula Wiseman Book." • Summary: A baby does not want to go to sleep, even as
everything else around her wishes her a good night. • ISBN 978-1-4424-1683-3 (alk. paper) • [1. Bedtime—Fiction. 2.
Babies—Fiction. 3. Night—Fiction.] I. Feiffer, Jules, ill. II. Title. • PZ7.F33346No 2012 • [E]—dc22 • 2010033776

NO GO SLEEP!

By **Kate Feiffer**

Illustrated by **Jules Feiffer**

A Paula Wiseman Book
Simon & Schuster Books for Young Readers
New York   London   Toronto   Sydney   New Delhi

One night when the stars were
out and the moon was bright,

a baby said,

"No go sleep!"

And the baby's mommy said, "It's time for you to close your eyes and think sweet thoughts."

And the baby's daddy said, "Put your head down
and fall fast asleep."

And the sun said,
"I've gone for the day.
When you wake up, I'll be back to play."

And the moon said, "Don't be scared.
I'll keep the night light for you."

And the stars said, "We will twinkle and sprinkle sweet dreams down to you."

And a car driving by said, "Beep, beep, sleep, sleep."

And the birds said, "We'll sing you a song."

And the frogs said, "We'll croak the chorus."

And the bunnies said, "We'll be listening."

And the owl said, "Who? Yes, me. I'll stay awake and watch over you."

And the tree said, "Close your eyes and listen
to the bustle of my rustle."

And the sheep said, "Count us one-two-three . . . and you'll fall asleep."

And the front door said, "I'm closed until morning."

And the goldfish said, "We won't swim away."

The dog said nothing. He was too sleepy.

And the shoes said, "We're just too tired to walk another step. Good night."

And a doll said, "I have my jammies on."

And the teddy bear said, "It's time to snuggle."

And the mommy said, "Please go to sleep."

And the baby said, "NO!"

And closed both eyes.

And fell asleep.

Night-night.
Sweet dreams.